ATTACK ON MINECRAFTERS ACADEMY

ATTACK ON MINECRAFTERS ACADEMY

THE UNOFFICIAL MINECRAFTERS ACADEMY SERIES

BOOK FOUR

Winter Morgan

Sky Pony Press
New York

Copyright © 2017 by Hollan Publishing, Inc.

Minecraft® is a registered trademark of Notch Development AB.

The Minecraft game is copyright © Mojang AB.

Sky Pony Press books may be purchased in bulk at special discounts for sales promotion, corporate gifts, fund-raising, or educational purposes. Special editions can also be created to specifications. For details, contact the Special Sales Department, Sky Pony Press, 307 West 36th Street, 11th Floor, New York, NY 10018 or info@skyhorsepublishing.com.

Sky Pony® is a registered trademark of Skyhorse Publishing, Inc.®, a Delaware corporation.

Minecraft® is a registered trademark of Notch Development AB.
The Minecraft game is copyright © Mojang AB.

Visit our website at www.skyponypress.com.

10 9 8 7 6 5 4 3 2 1

Library of Congress Cataloging-in-Publication Data is available on file.

Cover design by Brian Peterson
Cover photo by Megan Miller

Print ISBN: 978-1-5107-1815-9
Ebook ISBN: 978-1-5107-1824-1

Printed in Canada

TABLE OF CONTENTS

Chapter 1
THE FIRST DAY OF SCHOOL

J ulia only traveled out of the cold biome on rare occasions. She never felt the need to explore the rest of the Overworld when she could spend her days designing igloos and having snowball fights with her friends. Once she joined friends on a treasure hunt, which was supposed to be fun, but ended with her being trapped in a dark, musty stronghold, where an army of skeletons shot arrows at her with their bony hands, destroying her within seconds. She respawned in her bed. Later, her friends asked her if she was disappointed she missed out on unearthing treasure. To their shock, she confessed she was happy to respawn in her bed and have the adventure cut short. She liked the comforts of home.

Now, Julia stared at the acceptance letter to Minecrafters Academy. She'd applied on a lark. She'd never expected to get in. Julia wouldn't even have known about the Academy if it weren't for that super igloo she'd built. She had spent weeks constructing and perfecting an igloo, and as she worked on it, people passing through her frosty village stopped and asked her about her creation.

A pair of treasure hunters, trekking through snow in search of an abandoned mineshaft rumored to contain a slew of diamonds, stopped and gawked when they saw the igloo.

"You built that?" asked a man with black hair wearing a blue helmet, as he stood next to a friend who stood holding a pickaxe and wearing a gold helmet.

"Yes," Julia smiled proudly. "Why do you ask?"

The man in the gold helmet marveled, "It's incredible."

"We've been everywhere and we've never seen anything quite like it," added the man wearing the blue helmet, who introduced himself. "I'm Henry."

"I'm Max." The man wearing the gold helmet smiled. "And I have to tell you about this school that would be perfect for you. They have classes where you can learn to build even more incredible structures."

"It's only for the most skilled players, but I bet you'd have a chance," Henry said.

"How do you know about it?" Julia asked.

"Our friend Lucy is the headmistress," Max replied.

Julia listened to the details and then let the two treasure hunters tour the igloo.

"Wow," Max exclaimed as he entered the circular yet blocky white igloo. "You've done a fantastic job with the inside of the igloo." Max eyed the large wooden chests and the torches that were carefully placed in the spacious singular room.

Henry and Max excused themselves, thanking Julia for the tour and reminding her to apply to Minecrafters Academy, where she would learn how to build with other resources. Julia thought about applying for a long time and finally did. She knew it was a very competitive school, so she sent in the application expecting to be rejected.

When she was alerted that she was accepted and was to start classes the following day, her heart beat fast. She wondered if she could back out, but she told herself that it was important to try new things. Like the treasure hunt she had taken with her friends she tried it and realized it wasn't for her, but she never regretted going on the treasure hunt.

Julia stocked her inventory with all the required supplies requested Minecrafters Academy, and also added a lucky sword extra emeralds, and wheat, as well as other resources for trading.

Julia was offered two options to travel to Minecrafters Academy. She could TP there or she could travel through the Overworld. After studying the map, which highlighted mines, temples, and other spots where you could find treasures, she chose to TP to the school. She didn't want to risk battling any hostile mobs en route to the academy. Julia would be the first to admit she was the probably the worst fighter in the Overworld. Every time she was accidentally out past dark and saw a zombie or a skeleton, she'd freeze, making herself a target for the vicious hostile mobs of the night.

Julia TPed to the entrance of the school, and was greeted by a woman with yellow hair and glasses, who said, "You must be Julia."

"How did you know?" Julia stared at her with her piercing green eyes, and pushed her flaming red hair from her face.

"I've heard a lot about you," the woman said. "I'm Lucy. I'm the new headmistress."

"I found out about this school from your friends, Henry and Max." Julia was excited to meet the headmistress.

"Julia," a familiar voice called out. Julia turned around and saw Henry sprinting toward her and Max trailing behind him in the distance.

"Henry and Max. What are you doing here?" Julia raised her voice.

"They are teaching here this year," said Lucy. "I'm lucky to have them. In fact, you have Henry's survival class and Max's modding class on your schedule today."

"That's great." Julia smiled. She was relieved to know people at the Academy.

"I'm going to have Carla, the director of student life, take you to the dorms. You need to get settled in your room and meet your roommate," said Lucy, and she called Carla over.

Carla, dressed in a MInecrafters Academy shirt, walked over to Julia and smiled. "Welcome! I hope you're enjoying your first day."

"Yes, but I just got here. This is exciting, but slightly overwhelming," Julia said.

"That's normal. Everyone feels like that on the first day of school," Carla said.

Julia took a deep breath as she entered the dorms. She was just getting used to the idea that she'd be living in a snowless biome, and now Carla was about to introduce her to her roommate.

"This is Hallie." Carla introduced Julia to a girl with blue hair and daisy hair clip. She wore knee-high socks and a plaid dress.

"Do we have to wear a uniform?" Julia asked.

"No." Hallie spoke very softly, almost inaudibly. "Why?"

"Oh." Julia smiled. "I saw your plaid dress and thought it looked like a uniform."

"Don't make fun of me or else," Hallie mumbled so that Carla couldn't hear.

Carla excused herself. "Have a great time getting acquainted. And remember you both have Henry's Survival Skills class soon." She left.

Julia apologized. "I'm sorry. I wasn't making fun of you. You'll have to excuse me. I'm used to living alone and this is new for me."

Hallie snapped, "How do you think I feel?"

Julia looked over the list of resources she needed for Henry's survival class and asked Hallie, "Do you want to walk to class with me?"

"No, I have things I need to do before I go," Hallie said quietly.

Julia was worried about the other students at Minecrafters Academy and was scared she wouldn't make any friends. As she entered the class, Hallie spotted two girls standing next to an open chest. The girl with blond hair and wearing a red shirt smiled at Julia and invited her to join them.

"Hi, I'm Emma and this is Mia."

Mia's black hair covered most of her left eye, and she said, "Henry told us we have to pack this chest with what we believe are the most essential weapons and potions for survival."

Julia quickly scanned her inventory for everything needed to survive. "Did he say where? Which biome? I know in the cold biome you'll need a lot of different supplies because we don't have as much wood as the other biomes, and also except for a wolf or maybe a polar bear, we don't have too many animals around to hunt for food."

Julia didn't see Henry standing behind her as she spoke. "Wow, that's an excellent point, Julia," Henry commended her.

Julia was startled. She didn't want to be the teacher's pet, but she was also proud to be taken seriously. "Are you asking us about basic survival?" Julia wanted clarification for Henry's assignment.

Henry lectured the class on different types of survival and what they needed to know. As he broke the class into teams, Julia was happy when Emma and Mia asked her to work with them again.

"You really impressed Henry," Mia said as they worked on a project where they would each choose a different potion and use it, and everyone in the class had to guess which one the group used.

"We can't splash the potion of invisibility on ourselves or people will get it right away. We have to choose something a bit trickier," Emma suggested.

Mia and Julia agreed, but Julia couldn't focus on the assignment. She was too busy staring at Hallie, who entered the class late and worked alone. She stood in the corner, holding a vial of potion.

Before the class had time to share their potions with the group, the bell rang, and Henry said, "Remember who you were working with and what potions you were going to use, we will start the next class with presentations."

Emma asked Julia if she wanted to join them for lunch. Julia agreed, but she also kept an eye on Hallie.

"Why do you keep staring at that girl?" Mia asked.

"That's my roommate, Hallie. There's something strange about her. I'm keeping an eye on her." As Julia said this, she noticed Hallie walking in the opposite direction of the dining hall.

"It looks like she's skipping lunch," Emma remarked.

Julia stood as she watched Hallie walk into a wooded area and disappear into a thick patch of leaves. "I wonder where she's going."

"Let's follow her," Mia said.

Chapter 2
A SPECIAL INVITATION

Emma was the first to enter the thick patch of leaves to search for Hallie. Mia pushed the leaves away and saw Emma walking into the forest.

"Do you see anything?" Mia asked as she stood behind Emma.

"Yes, I see an opening to a cave," Emma said.

Julia had one foot into the wooded area when a voice called out her name, and she turned around to see Lucy.

"Julia, did you forget there's a mandatory assembly today before lunch? That means everyone must attend." Lucy walked over to them.

Emma and Mia emerged from the wooded area, as Julia replied, "We wouldn't miss it. Thanks for reminding me."

"What were you doing, entering the forest?" Lucy suspiciously eyed the trio.

"We were looking for an arrow we had lost," Emma fibbed.

"Well, you'll have to look for it later." Lucy walked toward the main hall. "Follow me to the assembly."

Julia wanted to confess. She wanted to tell Lucy that her roommate, Hallie, was missing the assembly and was in a cave hidden behind the trees, but she didn't say anything and followed Lucy toward the main hall. The main hall was crowded with students. Carla was addressing the group at the podium and welcoming them all to MInecrafters Academy.

"Tonight there will be a large feast on the grass outside the dorms. Get there early. We don't want to stay out late, because we don't want to battle hostile mobs after a large dinner. We don't want to get indigestion." Everyone chuckled and Carla said, "Here is our new headmistress Lucy, and she has some incredible news."

Lucy stood on the podium. As Carla stepped down, Lucy said, "I'm pleased to announce that our school was chosen to compete in the Minecraft Academic Olympics."

Cheers roared throughout the crowded auditorium.

"The prestigious Minecraft Academic Olympics will showcase all the skills students learn while at Minecrafter's Academy. However, there is some bad news. Although this is an elite school that chooses only the most serious students, the Olympics will only allow three students from the school to represent Minecrafters Academy. Tomorrow, we will host tryouts. Please let us know if you wish to try out for the Academic Olympics. I know it's just the first day of school and you're all still adjusting, but next week we have to let the Olympic Committee who we are sending to the competition."

The assembly ended. Mia, Julia, and Emma walked toward the dining hall. Mia was excited about the Olympics. "I have to try out. This sounds amazing."

"What do you want to try out for?" Julia asked.

"Potions. I got accepted due to my skills as an alchemist. After lunch, I'm going straight to the lab to start working on the potions."

"The lab? What about finding out where Hallie is?" Julia asked.

"She wasn't at the assembly," Emma said.

"Good," Mia said. "That's one less person to compete with. Headmistress Lucy said they could only send three people."

"Wouldn't it be great if we were all chosen? We could go to the Academic Olympics together!" Emma said.

"You're not going to get chosen if you slack off and spend your afternoon chasing after Julia's roommate. Everyone in this school wants to be a part of the competition, so you're going to have to put in a lot of effort," Mia said.

"I want to represent the school as a builder," Julia said. "I can make a fierce igloo."

Emma confessed, "I think I also want to try out for alchemy, but it seems like you have that covered, Mia."

"We can both try out," Mia said, adding, "but only one of us can get in."

"What was the skill that got you into Minecrafters Academy?" Julia asked Emma.

Emma put her head down. "I'm a warrior," she said softly.

"A what?" Mia asked.

"A warrior. I am an extremely skilled fighter and have a perfect aim with an arrow, but I don't want to fight. I grew up in a very dangerous part of the Overworld and due to circumstances beyond my control, I also spent a large portion of my time in the Nether. It was there that I perfected my skills," Emma said. "But I'd rather mix potions."

"I wish I could be a skilled fighter," Julia said. "I am the worst. If I see any hostile mob, I just freeze. I'm the easiest target in the Overworld."

"I think you should try out to represent the school as a fighter," Mia said. "Alchemy isn't easy and it takes a long time to perfect. If you have a skill you excel at, you should just work on being the best at that skill."

"I guess you're right," Emma said.

"Emma." Mia smiled. "If you'd like, I will teach you all I know about alchemy, but only after the tryout."

"Deal," Emma said.

Julia was relieved that her two new friends weren't in a competitive battle to represent the school as the best alchemist. However, although she wanted to be a part of the competition, she also wanted to head into the woods and find out what Hallie was doing in the cave.

"I don't think you can head straight to the lab," Emma reminded Mia. "Don't we have the modding class?"

"Oh, right." Mia looked at the schedule. "After that I'm in the lab."

"And if Hallie doesn't show up in the modding class, I'm going to look for her," Julia said.

The girls finished their lunch and made their way toward the main building that housed the modding class. Julia smiled when she saw Max standing in front of the class.

"Mods are a way of taking control and changing our landscape and capabilities." Max lectured them on Java code and made them brainstorm lists of ideas of what mods they'd like to create. Julia didn't want to appear distracted, but she spent the entire class staring at the door, waiting for Hallie to walk through it. When the class ended and Hallie didn't show up, Julia excused herself from Emma and Mia and walked toward the forest.

"Wait up," a familiar voice called out.

Julia turned around and saw Emma sprinting toward her. "Aren't you going to work on perfecting your fighting skills?"

"I heard what you said about being scared when you encounter a hostile mob. I was worried about you," Emma said. "What if Hallie is dangerous? How will you defend yourself?"

"I'm not sure," Julia said.

Emma and Julia walked toward the forest. Suddenly they heard a loud explosion.

"What was that?" Emma cried.

Julia turned and saw smoke. "I don't know, but we have to find out."

Chapter 3
EXPLOSIONS

Two students sprinted past Julia and Emma. Julia called out to them, "What happened?"

"Somebody blew up the main hall," the student hollered.

"What? Are you serious?" Julia didn't need to hear a response. She saw the rubble through the thick smoke that coated the campus. "Why would somebody do that?"

"I have no idea." Emma was equally perplexed.

"We have to find Mia." Julia looked for Mia in the crowd of students that filled the lawn outside the remnants of the main hall.

"I hope she wasn't in a lab in the main hall," Emma said.

"Since nobody spent the night here, everyone is going to respawn in their hometown and will have to TP here," Julia said.

"Wow," Emma said. "I never thought of that, but look." Emma pointed to three people who TPed in front of them. "You're right."

Julia and Emma heard Mia call out their names, and they ran toward their friend.

"Are you okay?" Emma asked.

"It was awful. I escaped but so many people were destroyed in the explosion." Mia tried to catch her breath.

"You're lucky you got out," Julia said.

"I have to tell you about something strange that happened right before the explosion." Mia spoke slowly, but was interrupted when Lucy called out to the crowd.

Lucy clutched a megaphone and said, "Everyone, there's an emergency assembly. Go into the auditorium."

Emma was apprehensive about entering the auditorium; she worried that it would be the next building to explode. She reluctantly entered the building. The students gathered in the auditorium, waiting to hear Lucy speak. Lucy walked up to the podium and addressed the group. "Today, we had a horrible occurrence on our campus. This was an incredibly difficult first day at MInecrafters Academy."

A student called out, "Do you know who blew up the Main Hall?"

Lucy shook her head. "I wish I had more answers. We are currently investigating the explosion. We have no idea if it was intentional or accidental. I know that many students were working in the Main Hall, preparing for tomorrow's tryouts for the Minecraft Academic Olympics. We aren't sure if one of them accidentally blew up the Main Hall."

Julia hoped that it was all an accident, as she scanned the auditorium for Hallie, who had been missing for most of the day.

Lucy continued. "There will be a dinner on the great lawn shortly. We will also gather a group of students who will work on redesigning and constructing the Main Hall."

Julia wanted to be a part of this team of students, but she also didn't want to be distracted as she prepared for the tryouts.

Lucy said, "The Minecraft Academic Olympic tryouts will continue tomorrow. Everything is back to normal."

As she spoke, four green creepers silently lurked behind her. The students didn't have time to warn the headmistress, because before she could utter another word, the creepers ignited and Lucy disappeared.

"Lucy!" Henry and Max called out and bolted out of the auditorium.

The crowd of students were shocked. They awkwardly made their way to the great lawn for the introductory dinner. Julia could hear students questioning if the dinner was still happening. As they exited the building, the great lawn was set up for a feast.

Julia asked Mia, "What happened when you were in the Main Hall? What was the strange story you wanted to tell us?"

Mia replied, "Your roommate, Hallie, was in the Main Hall. She was working beside me at another brewing stand. She kept looking over at me. I thought she wanted to talk to me, but every time I said something she seemed annoyed. She brewed a potion, placed it in her inventory, and sprinted out of the Main Hall. I thought that was strange. But what was even weirder was the minute she bolted out of the room, the Main Hall exploded."

"Do you really think she had something to do with the explosion?" Emma asked.

"I'm not sure, but I think we should tell Lucy. It might be a coincidence, but I think it's odd that she ran out of the lab seconds before the building exploded, don't you?"

Julia and Emma agreed that it was strange behavior, but they also knew it didn't mean Hallie blew up the Main Hall. However, everyone thought they should alert Lucy to Hallie's suspicious behavior.

The trio walked into the building where the faculty was housed and walked up the stairs to Lucy's room. Henry and Max stood by her door. Henry asked them, "If you've come to check on Lucy, she's fine."

Max said, "This has been some day, right?"

"Lucy will be at the dinner soon," Henry said. "She is just resting. We'll let her know that you came to visit."

They could hear Lucy's voice, "Who are you talking to?" she asked Henry and Max.

Lucy walked out of the room, and Julia wanted to rush over to her and tell her all about her suspicious roommate, but she didn't. Instead she took a rather loud deep breath when she saw Hallie walk out of Lucy's room.

Chapter 4
THE FEAST

"**A**re you heading to the feast?" Lucy asked.

"Yes," Julia replied, as she stared at Hallie.

"Great, let's all go down together. Carla worked very hard putting this evening together and I want to make sure it goes well," Lucy said.

Emma, Mia, and Julia followed Lucy, Max, Henry, and Hallie to the feast. When they were out of earshot, Julia said to her friends, "What is happening?"

"Maybe we were wrong about Hallie," Emma said. "Maybe she's a good guy."

"I'm not sure about that," Julia said. "I wonder if they're all bad."

"That sounds mad," ia said. "I think we shouldn't make up stories. Let's just enjoy the feast and then spend the rest of the evening practicing for the tryouts. I think it would be totally fun if we all got to participate together."

They all agreed they would try their best to get into the Academic Olympics, and would stop focusing on Hallie and if she was a part of a sinister plan.

Carla had plates of chicken, cake, and apples. Julia was excited to eat chicken. She never ate meat in the snowy biome. Emma was thrilled when she saw they had imported Mooshroom Stew.

"Mooshroom Stew is my favorite," she exclaimed, "I was only on Mushroom Island once, and I had such a fantastic time."

The trio feasted as they introduced themselves to other students at the Academy. Julia was impressed with a student named Brad, who was one the best builders in the Overworld. She knew it would be a challenge to beat him in the tryout. Brad showed her pictures of all of the buildings he'd constructed in the Overworld.

"This one is amazing!" Julia said as she stared at a picture of a skyscraper. "It must be over one hundred floors."

"One hundred and one," Brad confirmed.

Julia almost choked on her chicken. "That's impressive." Julia started to worry that she might not make it into the Academic Olympics. When she was in the snowy biome, it was easy for her to think that she was the best builder in the Overworld because there wasn't any competition. But here she was, face to face with some of the most skilled students in the Overworld. Julia excused herself. She wanted to be alone.

Mia noticed Julia standing away from the crowd near a large tree. "What's the matter, Julia?"

"I don't think I'm going to try out for the competition," Julia confessed.

"What? Why?" Mia was shocked.

"I just met someone who is a much better builder. I don't think I have a chance of getting into Olympics, so why should I bother trying out?" Julia felt defeated, even though the competition hadn't even begun.

"You have to try out. Emma and I want to travel to the Academic Olympics with you."

"How are you so confident that you will get in?" asked Julia.

"I'm not, but I'm going to try my hardest and let the teachers decide. You should do the same," Mia said.

Julia knew she was right. Dusk was setting in and Lucy grabbed the megaphone, alerting everyone that they should head back to the dorms. "We have an early day tomorrow. First thing on the agenda are the tryouts."

As Julia walked back to the room, she saw Hallie sprint off toward the wooded area. She looked for Emma and Mia, but didn't see them, and was too afraid to follow Hallie on her own. Julia finally reached her room and crawled into bed. She looked over at Hallie's empty bed. In the morning, when she woke up, the bed was still empty and Julia wondered if Hallie had ever slept there.

Chapter 5
THE TRYOUTS

Julia looked out the window. Crowds of students stood in front of the building that housed the auditorium, and Julia realized people were already lining up for the tryouts. She spotted Emma and Mia walking across the lawn in the direction of the large line, and sprinted out of the dorms and toward her friends.

"Emma! Mia!" Julia called out.

"Julia," Mia smiled. "You're going to try out."

Julia looked at the line and saw Brad. "Yes, I realize that I have as good a chance as any other builder on this campus."

Emma looked up at the sky. "Did you feel that?"

Mia brushed a raindrop from her face. "Yes, it's raining."

"Look over there." Julia stood frozen in terror as two skeletons spawned inches from them.

Emma grabbed her bow and arrow, and with perfect aim, she struck both of the skeletons and destroyed them.

"Good job. Go pick up the bone and arrow they dropped," Mia said.

As Emma rushed to retrieve the dropped rewards, five more skeletons spawned, and Emma used her skills to defeat the new bony beasts that threatened them.

"Do you think this is a part of the competition?" Julia asked.

"I bet you're right," Mia said. "I could see this being a part of our tryouts."

Rain pounded down on the campus, and as it pooled on the soggy grass, Julia tried not to slip as she raced into the building to avoid a skeleton attack. As she sprinted into the auditorium, four skeletons aimed their arrows at her and she shrieked.

Julia froze. She didn't know what to do.

"Grab your bow and arrow," a voice called from behind.

Julia turned to see who spoke to her, as she moved her head, two arrows struck Julia, weakening her.

"Take this potion," the voice said. As she grabbed the potion, she realized it was Brad who was helping her. He was her main competition in the tryout, and here he was, selflessly saving her life.

Brad annihilated the skeletons as Julia drank the potion of healing. "Thanks."

"You can fight skeletons, too. You just have to put on some armor and use your bow and arrow."

Julia put on gold armor and clutched her bow and arrow, as Brad yelled, "Over there. I see more over there!"

She stared at the skeletons, took a deep breath, and aimed the bow at the bony beasts, striking one and destroying it.

"See? You can do it," Brad said.

Julia destroyed the second skeleton and felt more confident with her skills as a fighter.

"Do you think this is a part of the tryout?" Julia asked.

Brad replied, "If that's the case. I'm not helping you anymore. You're my biggest competition. I almost didn't show up today because of you."

"Really? I felt the same way," Julia said.

"Well, if this is the competition, let the best person win." Brad smiled.

A horde of skeletons stormed the auditorium. They chased Lucy, who pleaded for them to help her. Julia and Brad unleashed a barrage of arrows.

Julia hollered, "I don't think this is the competition."

Julia and Brad destroyed a few skeletons, but the remainder disappeared as the sun came out.

"Thank you, guys," Lucy commended Julia and Brad. "You did a fine job destroying the skeletons."

Carla rushed into the auditorium. "Lucy, are you okay?"

Lucy replied calmly, "Yes, everything is fine. I guess it was an unexpected shower. We must go on with the tryouts. Please call everyone in and we will begin."

Julia looked over at Brad. She was standing inches from her competition, but she looked over at him and smiled. "Good luck."

"You too," he replied.

"Since you're the first people here, you can start," Lucy told Brad and Julia.

"We're both builders," Julia said.

"I know." Lucy smiled. "Just show me your best designs."

Julia pulled out a picture of her igloo and Brad showed Lucy the skyscraper. Lucy looked at each picture and paused. "Very good. I'll keep these. Thank you."

Julia saw Emma and Mia standing by the entrance, waiting to try out.

"I'll wait for you guys," Julia told her friends, but she was distracted when she saw Hallie walking across the campus. Julia followed her on the same path she had taken the day before. Julia walked into the wooded area, but turned around when someone called out her name.

Chapter 6
SPIDERS AND SILVERFISH

"Julia!"

Julia turned to see Emma and Mia sprint toward her. "How was your tryout?"

"I think it went well," Emma said.

"Mine too," Mia said.

"What are you doing?" Emma asked.

Julia put her finger over her lips to signify that they should keep their voices down and replied in a whisper, "Hallie's here. I bet she's in the cave."

"Let's find her," Mia said.

"Are you sure?" Emma seemed worried.

"Why not?" Mia questioned.

"I just worry that we'll get ourselves into a mess we weren't supposed to be involved with," Emma confessed.

"We have to help Minecrafters Academy," Julia reminded her. "We can't let Hallie get away with ruining the school."

"Slow down," Emma said. "We don't even know if Hallie is involved with anything."

"We have to stop talking and get into that cave. We could have lost her by now," Mia said as she disappeared into the thick leaves. Emma and Julia followed closely behind her.

Emma said, "Over here. The entrance is right here."

"Shhh!" Julia called out. "We don't want her to know we're here."

Mia pulled a torch from her inventory, and Emma said, "Good idea, I'll get a torch too."

The trio each placed a torch on the wall of the dimly lit cave. As the light shined, Emma shrieked.

"What's the matter?" Mia asked.

"Look down!" Emma pointed to the ground. The dirt floor was covered in silverfish. A few of the pesky insects crawled toward Julia, biting her.

"What are these?" Julia asked.

"Silverfish." Emma was shocked. "Have you never seen them?"

"Take this potion." Mia handed Julia a vial. "Drink it. You don't want to be weakened by the silverfish. They don't cause too much damage, but since there are so many of them here, they can be quite powerful."

Mia and Julia marveled when Emma grabbed a diamond sword from her inventory. Mia asked, "Is that an enchanted sword?'

"Yes," Emma replied while striking the sword against a sea of silverfish. "Help me. We have to stop these silverfish and find Hallie."

Julia and Mia plucked gold swords out of their inventory and joined Emma in the battle against the insidious insects. Julia heard a noise in the distance and looked up to see Hallie sprinting down the cave's dark hall.

"I see Hallie," Julia told the others. "We have to follow her."

Emma struck the remaining silverfish and sprinted behind Julia and Mia as they followed Hallie deeper into the dark cave.

"Watch out!" Mia cried as a pair of red eyes peered at them.

"I've got this," Emma said quite confidently as she swung her sword at the cave spider, destroying it with one hit.

"She's gone too far. We've lost her," Julia wailed as they walked down the hall.

"Maybe she's behind this door?" Mia stood in front of a wooden door.

"What do you think is behind it?" Julia asked.

"There's only one way to find out." Emma opened the door, and the trio entered a large room with a chest and a torch.

"It's a stronghold," Mia said.

Julia could see feet walking down the spiral staircase and said in a hushed whisper, "She's here."

"Should we open the chest?" Mia asked.

"No. We have to follow Hallie, and she's probably looted it anyway," Julia said.

The trio walked toward the spiral staircase. Before they reached the stairs, Mia grabbed her arm, letting out a piercing sound.

"Skeletons!" Emma adjusted her armor as she traded in her diamond sword for a bow and arrow.

Julia and Mia also aimed their arrows at the skeletons, but the minute they destroyed a skeleton, another seemed to spawn.

"She's getting away," Julia cried as she hit another skeleton and reached for the bone it dropped.

"We can't worry about Hallie. We have to stay alive." Mia tried to catch her breath. She was sprinting around the stronghold, attacking the skeletons.

"There are just a few left. We've got this," Emma said. Her arrows weakened the skeletons, and soon they were all destroyed.

Julia raced down the stairs. She didn't want to waste any time. She had to find Hallie.

"I see something!" Mia called out.

At the bottom of the stairs, the trio entered a spacious library laced with cobwebs and lined with bookshelves. Two large wooden chests sat in the middle of the library, which was lit by torches.

"Where did she go, Mia? I don't see anything." Julia scanned the library, but didn't see any other people.

Mia ran toward a dark corner of the library. "I don't know. She must have left."

"We have to find her." Julia looked around the library.

"I think I hear something," Mia said as she walked around the library, carefully inspecting each corner.

"Where?" Julia raced over to Mia.

Emma pointed to a stone staircase. "I hear something coming from down here."

The trio climbed down the stone staircase, and a person screamed out to them, "Leave me alone," and opened, then slammed shut a wooden door.

"Was that Hallie?" Julia asked.

"I don't know," said Emma, who raced toward the closed door and quickly opened it.

Behind the door was a large room lit by torches and an eerily empty jail cell.

"What is this place?" Emma stared at the jail cell.

"It's my home," a voice called out in the darkness.

"Who are you?" Mia asked.

There was no response. Julia walked toward the voice, reaching out for the shadowy figure.

"Stop!" the voice called out, but Julia just moved closer.

Chapter 7
POTIONS

"**D**o you know my friend Hallie?" Julia reached for the figure.

"I don't know Hallie," the voice called out. "Who's Hallie?"

Emma lit another torch from her inventory and walked toward Julia. The light illuminated a man's face. A man dressed in rags stood in the corner of the stronghold. A lone silverfish crawled up his leg. Emma slammed her diamond sword against the silverfish.

"Ouch," the man cried. "Why would you do that?"

"There was a silverfish. I'm sorry," Emma explained.

"I'd rather get bitten by an insect than have someone hit me with a sword. That really hurt."

"I'm sorry," Emma repeated.

"Who are you?" Julia asked.

"Why do you want to know? And what are you doing here? Shouldn't you be in school?" asked the man in rags.

"We were looking for my roommate," explained Julia. "We saw her enter the cave behind the campus."

"Minecrafters Academy," the man said and stared at the ceiling. "I remember that place. I used to be a student there."

"You were? When?" Mia asked.

"A very long time ago."

"Maybe you can help us," Emma said. "It appears that our school is in trouble. Someone blew up the Main Hall."

"Really? They destroyed the Main Hall? I learned all of my tricks in that building. What a shame." He frowned.

"What did you study at Minecrafters Academy?" Julia asked.

"You might not believe this, but at one time I was the best alchemist in the Overworld. But I gave it up."

"Why?" Mia asked, adding, "I'm also an alchemist."

"People became too greedy. There was also a person who wanted all of my potions and he would steal from me constantly."

"That's awful," Julia said.

"It's not that bad. I like being here where nobody can bother me." He smiled.

"Do you still brew potions?" Mia asked.

The old man walked toward a large chest. "Yes, I do." He lifted the lid of the chest, and Mia glared at the chest filled with labeled vials.

"You can make anything!" Mia exclaimed. "I need you to teach me. How did you find all of the resources to make these potions?"

"I'm not a teacher, and a good magician never tells anyone his tricks, right?" The old man's voice was tired.

"What's your name?" asked Julia. She was curious to ask Lucy, Carla, or another member of the faculty about this man who lived in the stronghold away from society.

"I'm Aaron," he said as he closed the chest.

"I'm Julia." She introduced her two friends.

Mia called out, "I think I hear something."

"Do you think it's Hallie?" Emma asked.

Julia smiled at Aaron. "It's been so nice meeting you, but we have to find my roommate, Hallie."

"Does she have blue hair and a flower hair clip?" Aaron asked.

"Yes, have you seen her?" Julia asked.

"Yes, she comes down here a lot, but I've never spoken to her," he replied.

"I wonder why she comes down here." Emma paced around the small room. "Is she using this place to plan something evil?"

"Do you think she's the one who blew up the Main Hall?" asked Aaron.

"We don't know. That's why we're down here," Julia said.

"I'm not sure your friend is doing anything bad. I think she uses this space to store chests. If you'd like, I can show you where I usually see her."

Julia wondered if she should trust Aaron. She worried that this might be a trap and that he could be working with Hallie. She asked, "Where do you usually see her?"

"By the entrance. She doesn't go too far into the cave. I've only seen her in the stronghold a couple of times," Aaron said.

"We will head toward the entrance," Julia said, thanking Aaron.

"Before you go," Aaron asked, "do you want to do a trade? I need food and I can sell you some of my potions for food."

Mia exclaimed, "Yes! I'd love some of those potions."

The gang looked through Aaron's inventory of potions, which included the potion of leaping, potion of luck, and other potions which would help them breathe underwater, have better night vision, and recover after an attack. The trio traded apples and wheat and filled their inventory with Aaron's potions.

"Why don't you come back to Minecrafters Academy?" Mia said. "There's a new headmistress. I bet she'd let you sell your potions on campus or even teach a class."

"I told you, I'm not a teacher. I'm also not looking to sell my potions. You've provided me with enough food to make it through the next few months, and I'm happy with that. I don't like to be around people."

"I get it," Mia said.

"Thank you for the potions," Julia said. "We must be on our way. We have to find my roommate."

"Good luck with everything. I hope you find out who blew up the Main Hall. I'd hate to see anything happen to the school." He smiled.

A thunderous boom rocked the stronghold. "What was that?" Julia's voice shook.

"I don't know." Aaron closed his chest of potions and hid it in a dark corner. "But it sounded like an explosion."

The trio walked up the stone stairs, through the library, and out of the stronghold. Julia turned around and was surprised to see Aaron trailing behind them. She thought he would have stayed in his part of the stronghold and wouldn't have joined them.

"Hallie!" Julia called out. Her blue-haired roommate stood by the entrance to the cave and stared at them blankly.

Julia rushed to her roommate, but Hallie sprinted out of the cave. Julia grabbed a potion of leaping, gulped it down, and was ready to pounce on Hallie when she heard a cry.

Emma wailed, "Help!"

Julia didn't realize she had sprinted past her friends. As she neared the cave's exit, she looked back at them. Creepers surrounded them. She had to help, but she knew it meant letting Hallie get away.

Chapter 8
SKELETONS IN THE CLOSET

Julia stared into one creeper's black blocky eyes. Aaron splashed potions on the creepers, destroying a few. Emma and Mia tried to quietly slip out of the cave before the creepers could ignite; they walked slowly and cautiously toward the exit, but more creepers spawned in front of them.

"I bet she created a creeper spawner," Julia said.

"We have to be very careful." Mia sprinkled potions on the creepers that crowded her path to the exit.

Even as Aaron spilled potions on the creepers, it was hopeless. They were outnumbered by green creepers and feared there was no escape.

"Let's just take it nice and slowly," said Emma, as she stood inches from the exit.

When the trio thought they were on the brink of a successful escape, the creepers detonated at once, rocking the small dimly lit cave.

The last thing Julia saw before she respawned in her bed was Aaron splashing a creeper with potion.

She looked over at Hallie's empty bed. Julia climbed out of her bed and she glanced at Hallie's half open closet. She wondered if she could gather any clues about Hallie by looking through the closet.

Julia opened the door to their room, and looked up and down the hall. She had to make sure Hallie wasn't anywhere near the room. Once she closed the door, Julia nervously walked over to Hallie's closet. The door was slightly open, and Julia peeked in. Three blocks of TNT were nestled in the corner behind a chest. Julia wasn't sure if she was imagining things. She opened the door completely and began to closely inspect the closet.

The closet contained a chest filled with gold bars, and behind the chest were definitely blocks of TNT. There was another chest deeper in the closet, but Julia heard a noise and jumped up.

"Julia?" Hallie asked in a quiet but angry mumble.

"Yes?" Julia wanted to question Hallie. She wanted to know why Hallie got to play by her own rules and constantly missed class and left the campus to head to the cave. She wanted to know what Hallie was hiding in the cave. Instead, she said nothing.

"Were you in the cave earlier today?" Hallie began her interrogation but it was so low and muffled that Julia wasn't quite sure what Hallie had actually asked.

"Yes," Julia said. "I was looking for you. I saw you leave the campus and enter the cave. I wanted to see if you were all right."

"You brought friends with you?"

"Yes, they didn't want me going alone."

"Why did you follow me?"

"We were worried about you."

"Worried about me? Your friends don't even know me." Each time Hallie spoke, she got closer to Julia.

"I was the one who was worried. They were there to help me find you. We saw you walk into the woods and we were curious."

"Stop being curious."

"Okay." Sweat ran down Julia's forehead.

"Don't look for me anymore. Leave me alone." Hallie stood inches from Julia's face now, so each word was extremely audible.

"But I promise that I was just worried about you."

"Don't worry about me." Hallie was almost on top of Julia. She could feel Hallie's breath on her face.

"I won't," Julia said, adding, "and I don't like feeling threatened."

"It wasn't a threat," Hallie said and quickly left the room.

Julia caught her breath. She didn't realize her heart was beating as fast as it was. She hated confrontation, and she also didn't know what Hallie was planning. She was worried for herself and the rest of the students at Minecrafters Academy. Julia had to tell Lucy about the TNT, but then she remembered Hallie leaving Lucy's room. Julia wondered if Lucy was involved in this, and if she might potentially be working with Hallie.

Emma and Mia entered Julia's room. Mia said, "I hope Aaron is all right."

Emma noticed Julia was upset. "What's wrong? You're as pale as a ghost."

"I just had a confrontation with Hallie. She told me that I should never go looking for her again. She also was upset that you were there," Julia spit out in one breath.

"That must have been awful," Emma said.

"It was. Before she came in, I made a crazy discovery," Julia took a deep breath.

"What did you find?" Mia asked.

"She has bricks of TNT in her closet, and she also has a chest filled with gold bars."

"TNT? How many bricks?" Emma said.

"Just three."

"I wonder if she used the rest to blow up the Main Hall."

"There was another chest in the back of the closet, but I couldn't get to it," Julia said.

"Let's look at it now," Emma suggested.

"Seriously? How? She just confronted me. If she comes in and sees me going through her closet, she will go nuts," Julia's heart began to race at the thought of Hallie catching her rummaging through her closet.

Mia pulled out a bottle of potion. "She'll never know. We'll become invisible."

"I'm not sure that's the best idea," Julia protested.

"No, it's a great idea," Emma declared.

"We need as much evidence on Hallie as we can get. Then we can go see Lucy and tell her what's going on," Mia explained.

"Hallie could be working with Lucy. Remember we saw her coming out of her room?" Julia reminded them.

"I think we have no choice. We have to open that chest. It could contain a vital clue," said Mia as she splashed the potion of invisibility on herself and walked into Hallie's closet.

Emma also splashed the potion on herself and joined Mia on the search through Hallie's closet.

"I see the TNT," Emma said.

"I can almost reach the chest," Mia said.

Julia stood by the door and watched for Hallie. She couldn't get enough courage to splash the potion on herself. Luckily she didn't, because Hallie opened the door.

Chapter 9
LUNCH IS OVER

"You're back," Julia said quite loudly. She wanted Emma and Mia to know that Hallie had returned.

"Why is my closet door open?" Hallie asked as she walked over to the door and closed it.

Julia panicked that Hallie might hear Emma and Mia in her closet, and she let out a loud breath when the door closed without any issues.

"What's wrong with you?" Hallie stared at Julia. "You weren't looking through my closet, were you?"

"No," Julia lied, "of course not."

"You'd better be telling the truth," Hallie said.

"I think we have to go to class. I have Henry's survival class on my schedule. I know you do, too," Julia said.

"I'll see you there." Hallie left the bedroom.

Julia raced toward Hallie's closet, opening the door as her two friends' potion wore off and they became visible.

"We have to get out of here," Julia said.

Mia brushed her hair from her face, "Yes, we must go to Henry's survival class, but we also have to tell you what's in that chest."

"What?" Julia's heart skipped a beat as she led her two friends out of her room. She looked in both directions down the hall. She didn't want Hallie to see them exiting the room together.

"The chest is filled with enchanted books," Emma said.

"That's not so strange," Julia remarked.

"I know, but it's what we found behind the chest that worries us," Mia said.

"What?" Julia needed to know what was so worrisome.

"There is a huge hole in the wall behind the chest," Emma said.

"And it's filled with bricks of TNT," Mia said.

"What is she doing with all of that TNT?" Julia asked, although she knew her friends didn't have the answer.

"We have to tell someone at this school," Emma said.

"Maybe we can tell Carla," Julia suggested.

"That's a good idea," Mia said, "but we also have to get to class now. I know we are still being evaluated for the Academic Olympics. Even if our tryout was perfect, we're not going to get chosen if we start missing class."

"The school won't exist if we don't stop Hallie!" Julia exclaimed.

Mia and Emma stood in silence. Emma said, "You're right. We have to take this very seriously. There is a student at our school who is hoarding TNT. This is a big problem."

"It's true. Let's meet with Lucy after Survival Skills class," Mia said.

"If we survive," Julia said.

The group rushed into Henry's class. Henry addressed the class about the importance of potions in survival.

"For instance, not having an inventory filled with the adequate number of potions can be the difference between surviving and conquering a hostile mob or being destroyed." Henry asked them to work with their partners from the last class and to choose the potion the group felt was the most important for survival, the one potion they could never survive without.

Emma asked, "Should we use the leaping potion? It's very rare. I think that will impress Henry."

"I don't think this exercise is about impressing the teacher. We want to choose the potion that is most important for survival. I don't think, although it's rare and impressive to have in our inventory, that the potion of leaping is all that significant in everyday battles," explained Mia, who was a self-proclaimed potion expert and alchemist.

Julia was only half listening to the disagreement. She was too busy looking around the classroom for Hallie. "Guys, it looks like Hallie skipped class again."

"What a surprise," Emma said.

"We need to concentrate on this assignment," Mia reminded them.

Kaboom!

An explosion rocked the campus, and the classroom shook. Henry told the class to stay calm. "We will evacuate the classroom, but we need to stay focused and leave slowly. We can get very hurt if we panic."

"I told you we should have gone to Carla," Julia said.

"How could I know there would be another explosion?" Mia defended herself. "I just wanted to do the right thing and go to class. I want to succeed here."

"But we're not sure the school will even exist in a few weeks. We've been here two days and already two buildings have been destroyed. How many more are there? This school is in serious jeopardy," Julia said.

"There's no use discussing who is right or wrong. We need to tell Lucy what we found in Hallie's room," Emma said.

Everyone crowded in the center of campus to access the damage. Julia stared at the dining hall, the second building destroyed.

"The dining hall," moaned Mia. "Where will we eat?"

"I'm going to miss the cake," Emma said.

"This isn't a time to joke." Julia pointed at Lucy in the distance. "We need to tell her what we found in Hallie's closet."

Julia sprinted over to Lucy, but stopped when she saw who was standing next to her.

Hallie was whispering something in Lucy's ear and they both stared at Julia.

Chapter 10
SEARCH AND FIND

Julia didn't know what to do. She stood in the center of the campus, staring back at Lucy and Hallie. She wondered if they were working together. Mia and Emma sprinted up behind Julia.

"What's the matter?" asked Mia.

"Look," Julia nodded to Hallie and Lucy. "I think we have a much bigger problem than we imagined."

"You have to talk to Lucy. Even if she's evil, you must confront her," Emma said.

Julia knew the only way she could get answers would be if she approached Lucy and questioned her.

Just then she overheard Henry talking to another teacher nearby.

"I can't believe someone destroyed the dining hall. It doesn't make sense. Why would anyone want to destroy the school?"

Julia chimed in on their conversation "You should ask your friend Lucy."

"What are you saying?" Henry was upset. "Lucy doesn't have anything to do with this."

"She is standing beside my roommate, Hallie. We found lots of bricks of TNT in her closet," explained.

"You have to tell Lucy," Henry said.

"But what if she's working with Hallie?" Emma said.

"I know Lucy, and I can tell you that she isn't working with Hallie," Henry declared.

The sound of thunder stunned the students. Rain began to pour down, and zombies spawned by the rubble that was once the dining hall.

"This is strange. It's the second time it rained in two days," Henry said as he put on armor and grabbed a sword.

Julia, Mia, and Emma also gathered their armor and swords, but Julia wasn't watching the zombies that lumbered toward them; she was too fixated on Lucy and Hallie. She wanted to see if they stayed to battle the vacant-eyed zombies or if they went to the dorms to get the TNT bricks from Hallie's closet.

Lucy grabbed her bow and arrow and aimed at the zombies, but Hallie was gone. Julia used this opportunity to reach out to Lucy. She sprinted across the wet lawn, slamming her sword against two zombies that stood in her path, and made her way to Lucy.

"Julia," Lucy said breathlessly. "This is certainly an intense battle. Why would you leave Henry? He's an expert fighter. He knows how to survive in situations like this one."

"I need to talk to you about Hallie," said Julia as three zombies circled them.

Lucy traded her bow and arrow for a diamond sword and struck one of the undead beasts, instantly destroying it. Julia fumbled with her sword as she struck the remaining zombies until they were destroyed. As more zombies spawned, the sun came out and they disappeared.

"We're safe." Lucy let out a deep breath.

"No, we're not," Julia said.

"What are you talking about, Julia? Are you threatening our campus? Your roommate, Hallie, has met with me twice. She is worried about your behavior and thinks you might be behind these attacks."

Julia gasped, "What? Are you serious?"

Emma, Mia, and Henry sprinted over to Julia and heard Lucy say, "Yes, Hallie is very worried. She wanted me to alert Carla and the rest of the faculty about your behavior. She said you follow her around campus and search through her belongings."

"We did go through her closet," confessed Emma, "and we found a large amount of bricks of TNT."

"What?" Lucy was shocked.

"Yes, we also found a chest filled with gold bricks. I'm not sure if someone is paying her, but I think we should consider her a suspect," Julia said.

"At this minute everyone on campus is a suspect," Lucy said.

Henry said, "Lucy, I think we should have a talk with Hallie."

"I agree, but I'm not going to place blame on any student until I have concrete evidence and hopefully a confession," Lucy said.

Carla rushed over to the group, "I just saw one of our students carrying blocks of TNT and I tried to stop her, but she splashed a potion of invisibility of herself."

"Was it Hallie?" Lucy asked.

"How did you know?" Carla said.

As Lucy replied, a loud explosion was heard throughout the campus.

"What was that?" Carla asked.

"It looks the smoke is coming from the direction of the auditorium," Henry said.

The group sprinted toward the smoke. Lucy looked over at Julia. "I'm sorry I didn't believe you."

"We have to stop her," Julia said.

Everyone agreed, but there was one major problem. After the smoke settled, they searched the campus for Hallie, but she was nowhere to be found.

Hallie had vanished from MInecrafters Academy without a trace.

Julia walked back to her empty dorm room. Hallie had taken all of her stuff. Even the closet full of TNT was empty. Julia hoped this was the end of Hallie, and there would be peace on campus.

Lucy held an emergency assembly on the great lawn. This time there was no podium, and although the location was informal, what was discussed was quite important. Lucy said, "I'm sorry to make this announcement, but we will not have classes this week. Everyone must work on rebuilding the Main Hall, the dining hall and the auditorium."

Julia was excited to work on the project, but she was also upset that her academics wouldn't continue until the school was rebuilt. Mia stood next to Julia and asked, "Should I ask a question about the Academic Olympics?"

"No, this isn't the time," Julia advised.

Emma agreed. "We have bigger issues."

"At least Hallie is gone. Maybe this means things will finally get back to normal," Mia said.

Lucy concluded the emergency assembly and walked toward Julia, Emma, and Mia. "I need to talk to you guys," Lucy said.

"I'd love to help rebuild the campus," Julia said.

"I'm sorry, but I need you for another project," Lucy said.

"What type of project?"

"I have Hallie's address in the Jungle. I need you to go find her and bring her back."

"Alone?"

"No. You should bring your friends Mia and Emma," Lucy replied.

Mia suggested, "We should go see Aaron before we go and replenish our supply of potions."

"Aaron?" Lucy asked.

"He's an old man we met living in the stronghold right near the campus," Mia explained.

"We met him when we were searching for Hallie," Julia said.

"I haven't heard that name in a long time. There was once a student here by that name. We were schoolmates in fact, but he's been missing for years," Lucy said.

"I bet it's the same guy. He said he used to go school here," Julia said.

"I think we should all see him, before you leave on your journey," said Lucy.

The trio walked into the thick patch of leaves with Lucy. They were going to find Aaron.

"It's right here," said Emma, but the cave was missing.

"Where's the cave's entrance?" Julia asked.

"This is definitely the spot," Mia said.

"This is so strange," Julia remarked.

A voice called out in the distance. "Are you looking for me?"

Chapter 11
THE JUNGLE

"Aaron," Lucy called out gleefully.

"Hello, my old friend," Aaron said.

"We need potions," Mia said.

"That's not the only reason we're here," Lucy said. "We need your help. I want you to travel to the Jungle with Julia, Mia and Emma."

"The Jungle?" Aaron shrugged. "I'm an old man. I can't travel to the Jungle. My days as an adventurer are over."

"You still have the strength to help. I know you do," Lucy said.

Aaron blushed. "You always know the right things to say."

Mia added, "If you don't have the energy, just drink lots of potions of strength. I'm also sure that anyone who has the ability to gather all of the ingredients to brew those potions is quite strong."

Lucy smiled. "I think you'll be in good hands, Aaron. This is very important to me and to Minecrafters Academy. I'm also going to go with you guys. I think we have to find Hallie as soon as possible."

"Wow!" Aaron exclaimed. "You're coming too?"

"Yes," Lucy replied. "I'm leaving one of the faculty, Carla, in charge of the campus."

Julia looked up at the sky. Dusk was approaching. "We should leave soon, because we don't want to travel at night."

Lucy grabbed a map from her inventory, and pointed out where Hallie's house was in the Jungle. "She lives in this small village next to a Jungle temple."

The four friends followed Lucy through the woods and toward the Jungle. After walking through meadows and forest biomes, Lucy suggested they build a house in a grassy patch outside a swamp.

Julia wasn't used to constructing homes from wooden planks; she usually built her homes with snow. "This is much easier," Julia pointed out as she placed the wooden planks on the ground and built the home's structure within minutes.

"You're doing a great job," Lucy said.

"Thanks," Julia replied, but threw down the wooden planks when she heard Mia let out a bloodcurdling scream.

"Mia?" Emma screamed.

"Help," Mia hollered. "Please help me."

Julia sprinted toward the sound of Mia's voice, and found her friend in the middle of an intense battle with a witch. The purple-robed witch clutched a bottle of potion and stood inches from a terrified Mia.

"Use your potions," Aaron called. "You can do this."

Julia had never seen a witch, and it was a lot scarier than she'd imagined. She wanted to help her friend, but she was also scared of becoming the witch's next victim. Julia quickly grabbed her bow and arrow and aimed at the witch. The arrow struck the witch's leg and irritated the old woman, who lunged at Mia with her potion. The witch doused Mia with poisonous potion that weakened her.

Aaron sprinted toward the witch, splashing a mixture of two potions on the venomous witch, which greatly slowed the witch's movements. "Shoot your arrows!" Aaron ordered the others as he rushed to Mia's side and gave her a potion that reversed the damage from the witch's poison.

Mia drank the potion. "Thank you. I feel so much better." She ducked from the arrows and struck the witch which her gold sword, destroying the black-hatted cauldron-brewing beast.

"We have to finish building the house," Lucy said, staring at the evening sky and the large full moon, as a bat flew by them. "Yes, we have to work incredibly fast. I don't want us to be distracted by any more battles."

Julia was placing the windows on the house when she heard an unfamiliar noise. "Does anybody hear that? It sounds like something is bouncing."

"Shhh," Lucy said. "Julia, stop building."

"I hear it too," Aaron said.

"Slimes!" Mia cried.

Six green blocks bounced toward them. Emma was the first to slay a slime with her diamond sword, but the slime wasn't destroyed; it broke into smaller chunks. The others gathered around the smaller pieces of slime, slamming them with their swords.

Julia struck a slime. She felt someone standing behind her, assuming it was one of her friends, so she struck another slime without turning back. As she plunged her sword deep into the green slime, she felt incredibly tired and her body seemed to move in slow motion.

Emma gasped and ran toward Julia, clutching her diamond sword.

"Please don't hurt me," Julia cried out, but her voice was low and she could barely get the words out. She was confused and wondered why her good friend Emma was ready to attack her, until she heard Aaron say something about a witch. Julia realized it was a witch who stood behind her, ready to annihilate her if her friends didn't help. Julia didn't have the energy to pull a potion from her inventory or strike the witch with her sword; she just stood in front of the witch feeling incredibly weak and helpless.

Emma sprinted toward the witch, ripping into her with a diamond sword, but the witch shrugged off the attack and drank a potion, which replenished her energy. Julia wanted to move away from the witch, but she couldn't. The witch splashed another potion on Julia as Emma lunged again at the witch with her sword. The witch was slaughtered, but not before it managed to destroy Julia.

Moments later, Julia respawned on the Minecrafters Academy campus and cautiously scanned the horizon. The sky had grown eerily dark. She felt a pit in her stomach as a three-headed shadow slowly emerged from behind the school building. It occurred to Julia that she might not make it back to her friends alive.

Chapter 12
BUILD A TRAP

When Julia finally appeared in the wooden house by the swamp, she was greeted with both excitement and relief.

"Are you okay?" Emma asked. "Don't worry. The witch was destroyed. We built onto the house to make it safer and made beds for all of us."

Julia's face was pale. Her fiery red hair seemed even brighter against her snow-white skin. She let out a sigh as she said, "We have to go back to Minecrafters Academy now."

"What? We can't!" Lucy protested "What's happening there? Is everyone okay?"

The barrage of questions overwhelmed Julia. All she could spit out was one word: "Wither."

"The Wither? Is there a Wither attacking the school?" Lucy asked.

Julia shook her head.

"She looks very weak." Aaron walked over to Julia and handed her a potion to regain her strength.

Julia took small sips. She started to feel a bit stronger and began to speak. "It's in the middle of the campus. It was shooting these intense fiery skulls. I've never seen anything like it before. I've only heard stories about the Wither or the Ender Dragon, but when you see them up close, it's really horrible." Tears streamed down Julia's face as she described the Wither.

Lucy paced the length of the small house. "This is awful. We must all TP there right now."

"First, we have to put on our armor," Emma reminded them. "I've fought the Wither many times and it's incredibly tricky. We can't just go there and blindly fight this powerful mob. We must have a plan."

"What should we do?" Julia asked Emma. "You've defeated the Wither before, so you must have some insight."

"We have to trap it. This is where you will be incredibly helpful, Julia. When we get back to campus, I will take the others and lead them into the battle with the Wither. You must construct a bedrock structure where you can trap the Wither. We will lead the Wither to that structure. Does everybody get the plan?" Emma asked the group.

"Yes." Lucy spoke for the group as she ordered everyone to TP.

The group TPed and landed in the belly of the action. They immediately ducked when three flaming wither skulls shot in their direction.

"Duck," cried Emma as she raced toward the Wither, striking the three-headed beast with an arrow. This infuriated the beast, as it wasn't accustomed to getting struck by an arrow. The Wither stared at Emma with its three heads and blasted her with wither skulls. Emma sprinted from the skulls, narrowly avoiding a fiery demise.

Mia, Aaron, and Lucy sprinted toward Emma, aiming their arrows at the Wither. They each struck a part of the muscular mob.

"We're weakening it!" Mia cheered.

"We have to lead the Wither to the bedrock structure Julia's building," Emma said weakly.

Aaron handed Emma a potion of strength. "Drink this, warrior. It will make you better."

Emma sipped the potion and eyed the campus for Julia. She wanted to know in which direction they should lead this flying pest that was tormenting the students and faculty at Minecrafters Academy.

Julia was building as quickly as she could. She worried because her inventory wasn't filled with enough bedrock to construct the final portion of the building. A familiar voice called out to her. "What are you doing? How can you build at a time like this?"

Julia looked up and spotted Brad sprinting toward her. "I have to build this. We need to trap the Wither in here. The only problem is that I don't have enough bedrock."

Brad pulled bedrock from his inventory. "I can help." He worked with Julia and they finished the building.

"We have to let Emma know that it's finished. She's leading the Wither toward this building and we're going to trap it. We have to leave the top open so the Wither can get trapped. Once the Wither is in the structure, we have to close it," Lucy told Brad.

"That seems rather difficult." Brad looked at the building and the large flying Wither in the distance. "People have been battling this Wither all night. I don't think trapping this beast will be an easy task."

"I know, but we have to try," Julia said. "Follow me. Let's find Emma and the gang."

Julia and Brad sprinted across the campus, dodging and ducking from the burning wither skulls that pelted down upon the great lawn. As they approached Emma and the others who shielded themselves behind a tree while they fought, Julia was startled when she saw Hallie rush past her.

"That's Hallie!" Julia called out.

"So?" Brad didn't understand why that was a big deal.

"She's back." Julia sprinted toward Emma.

Emma called out, "Did you finish the building?"

"Yes," Brad replied, "and we have just enough bed-rock left to construct a roof."

"Perfect," Emma exclaimed. "We will start leading the beast toward the building. You have to help us."

As Julia adjusted her armor, she announced, "Hallie is back. I just saw her on campus."

"What?" Lucy appeared surprised.

"Yes," Julia confirmed. "It was definitely her."

The Wither flew close to them. Aaron splashed a potion at the beast as the Wither shot fiery skulls that landed dangerously close to them.

"This tree isn't providing us with safety anymore," Emma said. "We must fight back and lead the Wither to the bedrock prison."

The group sprinted toward the bedrock structure as the Wither followed them, shooting a multitude of flaming skills in their direction.

"We're almost there," Julia called out.

The group was exhausted as they shot arrows at the Wither, leading the powerful beast to the bedrock structure.

"Do you think we can get it into the house?" Mia asked.

"We left a portion open. We can trap the Wither in there. You can battle it while Brad and I finish the structure and trap him," Julia said.

The Wither shot a fiery skull that hit Aaron. He was weakened. Another skull struck his leg, and Aaron was destroyed.

"Aaron!" Lucy cried out.

"I assume he'll respawn in the stronghold," Emma said.

Another skull struck Lucy, and she was also destroyed. Emma worried they might not have enough people to trap the Wither.

Julia and Brad shot their final arrows at the Wither as Emma and Mia led the Wither to the bedrock structure, Julia and Brad worked hard to finish it and trap the Wither. While Julia placed the final piece of bedrock, the Wither unleashed another round of wither skulls from its three heads. Two skulls hit Julia, instantly destroying her.

Julia awoke in her bed. She wanted to rush downstairs to help Brad place the final piece of bedrock, but she couldn't move. As she climbed out of bed, Julia gasped. Hallie stood above her. She pointed a diamond sword close to Julia's face. Glancing down, Julia spotted bricks of TNT lining the length of her bed. She looked up at Hallie and spit out a one-word question: "Why?"

Chapter 13
DISCOVERIES IN THE DUNGEON

"**D**on't move," Hallie threatened.

"But—" Julia barely got a word out before Hallie lunged and struck her with the diamond sword.

"You moved," Hallie screamed. "I told you not to move."

"What do you want from me?" Julia cried.

"You're coming with me. We're going to see some of your good friends." Hallie laughed.

"What did you do to my friends?" Julia was worried about them. She had no idea if Hallie was working alone or with a larger group. "Tell me now."

"Follow me," Hallie ordered as she held a diamond sword against Julia's chest.

"Where are we going? What happened to the Wither? Where are my friends?"

"You have so many questions." Hallie chuckled. "I can answer them, but I won't. You'll find out soon enough."

Julia followed Hallie out of the dorm room and down the stairs. It was daylight and the Wither was gone. The campus was eerily empty. Not one student walked across the campus.

"What happened to the students?" Julia asked.

"Stop asking questions."

Julia obeyed Hallie and walked behind her as they made their way through the woods dense with trees. Julia hoped she'd lose Hallie on a path covered with leaves, but Hallie was intent on keeping Julia her prisoner. She walked with the sword pointed at Julia, and Julia knew there was no escape. Hallie would whisper in Julia's ear which direction she should walk, and if Julia made a wrong turn she'd poke the sword against her chest.

"You're depleting my energy," Julia warned Hallie. "If you keep bumping your sword into my back, I will eventually respawn in my bed."

Julia regretted mentioning this to Hallie, as she realized this could have been an escape plan. However, she also wanted to find her friends. If she respawned in her bed, she might be safe, but she'd also be helpless in finding their location.

They passed the swamp and the small wooden structure she constructed with Lucy and the gang. For the first time in her life, Julia wished a witch would attack them and destroy Hallie. Yet they passed through the swamp biome without any incident. It was too light for hostile mobs to spawn. Julia wondered when night would set in, because the trip seemed to take forever. There were many times that Julia wanted to ask where they were going, but it was pointless. It seemed as if they had been walking forever when Julia spotted a temple in the distance. Hallie led her to the Jungle temple and said, "We're going into that Jungle temple."

Julia remembered Lucy mentioning that Hallie lived in a village in the Jungle, and realized Hallie must be incredibly familiar with this biome. Julia reluctantly followed Hallie deeper into the Jungle temple.

"We have to go downstairs," Hallie ordered.

Following Hallie down the stairs, Julia cringed when a pair of red eyes stared at them. Before Julia could scream, Hallie swung her sword at the cave spider, annihilating it with one strike.

"This is your new home." Hallie pointed to a prison cell.

Julia hated being trapped. Once a griefer covered the entrance to her igloo with snow and she couldn't get out. She'd spent two days frantically digging her way out of her home. Julia looked at the prison cell and sighed. She was plotting her escape when she heard someone call out her name.

"Brad?" She peered in to see Brad, Mia, Henry, and Lucy at the back of the prison cell.

Hallie opened the gate and locked it behind Julia. "Good luck, guys. If you ever get out of here, you'll be sad to find out that Minecrafters Academy is gone. I'm replacing it with my own school, where I teach people how to become villains." Hallie splashed a potion on herself and disappeared.

Scanning the small, dimly lit prison cell, Julia realized all her friends weren't there. "Where are Emma and Aaron?"

Lucy explained, "After we trapped the Wither, you were destroyed."

"I was destroyed before you placed the final brick," Julia interrupted.

Lucy seemed annoyed at Julia's interruption, and paced. "Once the Wither was captured, Hallie splashed a potion of weakness on us. She said if we didn't follow her, she'd detonate the TNT she'd placed around campus and would destroy every structure at Minecrafters Academy. We followed her, but Emma was able to escape, and Aaron never respawned on campus. We hope they'll rescue us, or at least save Minecrafters Academy."

"Why does she want to destroy the school?" Julia asked.

Brad said, "You heard her. She wants to turn it into a place that churns out evil villains."

"I know, but I just can't believe it," Julia had to come up with a plan that could help them escape.

"We need to get out of here," Mia said.

Henry looked through his inventory. "I think I have an escape plan."

"Really? Do you think you can get us out of here?" Lucy asked.

"Yes." Henry smirked.

"I have a plan too," Julia announced.

"Great," Brad said. "Let's hear them."

Chapter 14
HIDDEN IN THE MINE

"**Y**ou go first." Henry smiled. "I love when I learn from my students."

"But you're the survival expert," Julia said.

"This is no time to debate over who should go first," Lucy said. "Julia, tell us your plan."

"I think we should call Hallie down here and get her to open the gate. Once she does, we can each throw a potion on Hallie and overthrow her."

"Do you think she'll come down here?" Mia asked.

"There's only one way to find out," Julia said as she began to holler, the loudest, most powerful shrill scream anyone has ever heard.

Everyone covered their ears. They had never heard such a piercing, loud shriek. It wasn't a cry for help, but an intense scream that would have broken a glass or vial if it had been in the musty Jungle dungeon prison.

Hallie walked down the stairs, "What's that sound?"

Julia didn't stop. She kept screaming.

"What is wrong with you, Julia? Stop shouting!" Hallie demanded, but Julia wouldn't. Occasionally she would take a breath, but then she'd continue to unleash the harshest sound ever heard in the Overworld. Hallie opened the jail cell door and attempted to plunge her sword into Julia's stomach, but Julia continued to belt out her intensely caustic scream.

Henry, Lucy, Brad, and Mia leaped at Hallie. They struck her with swords and splashed her with potions until she disappeared.

"We have to get out of here," Lucy ordered, as the gang sprinted up the stairs and out of the Jungle. They raced back to the campus, but as they passed a mine they heard loud noises.

Julia stopped by the mine's entrance, and Lucy called out, "Don't stop, Julia. We have to keep going."

"It sounds like someone is in trouble in the mine. We have to investigate," Julia said.

"We can't. We have to get back to Minecrafters Academy," Lucy said.

Julia couldn't leave if she thought someone was in trouble, and she raced into the mine. She didn't turn back to see who was following her; she simply ran toward the sound of the cries.

"Julia," Aaron cried.

Julia was shocked to see Emma and Aaron battling Hallie. She quickly grabbed a sword from her inventory, ready to pounce on Hallie, when a barrage of arrows flew past her. Julia turned around, as Lucy, Henry, Brad, and Mia aimed their arrows and once again destroyed Hallie.

"Thankfully you showed up," Aaron let out a deep breath, "Hallie had her trapped down here."

Hallie respawned in front of them. "And now I'm going to trap you all down here."

"How?" Henry asked as he pointed his arrow at her.

Hallie smiled. "I have TNT bricks across the entire campus. If you don't stay here, I will set it all off and the entire campus will explode."

Lucy was the first person to shoot an arrow at Hallie, who was dumbfounded. Lucy called out, "You thought that threat would stop us from destroying you?" Lucy ordered Aaron and Henry to go back to campus. "I want to see if she's telling the truth. If she is, please remove the bricks of TNT."

Before Aaron and Henry could TP back to the campus, Hallie haphazardly constructed a portal to the Nether and vanished amidst a sea of purple mist. Julia eyed the fading portal and hopped on after Hallie. She let out a sigh of relief when she saw Emma standing next to her. She'd hate to emerge in the Nether alone with Hallie. She'd never been to the Nether before, and she knew Emma was an expert.

"Get out of here!" Hallie screamed at Julia and Emma, as she stood next to them on the portal, but there was no time to reply, because the portal dropped them in the center of the Nether, and a group of ghasts flew toward them.

Julia's heart felt as if it was beating out of her chest. The white blocky mob shot fireballs at them.

"Use your arrow," Emma instructed her and quickly added, "duck," as a fireball landed next to Julia's feet.

"She's getting away," Julia cried.

"Don't worry, we'll find her. We have to destroy the ghasts or they will follow us."

Emma's arrow pierced the white fire-breathing flying Nether mob and it vanished. She then aimed her arrow at another ghast, destroying it with one arrow. She told Julia to grab the dropped ghast tears. As Julia reached for them, Emma annihilated the final ghast and called out, "I see a Nether fortress."

"Do you think Hallie is in the fortress?" Julia asked.

"It seems likely that's where she'd be hiding. Also, there are great treasures there, and she would want them," Emma said.

Julia stared at the grand Nether fortress in the distance. Although she could see the fortress, she knew traveling toward it wouldn't be easy. As she looked at a lava waterfall, a vacant-eyed pig walked past them.

"Don't bother the zombie pigmen," Emma warned.

Julia knew there were too many rules to survive in the Nether. She was at a serious disadvantage because she knew none of them. Walking carefully toward the fortress along a stream of lava, Julia hoped she wouldn't accidentally break any rules.

Chapter 15
NOT IN THE NETHER

"I see her!" Emma pointed at a figure running in the distance.

"Are you sure that's her?" Julia asked. "I don't think that person has blue hair.'"

"Yes," Emma replied, dashing toward the fortress, "I swear it's her."

Steps from the fortress, two blazes rose from the ground, and flew high up as they shot fiery balls at them.

"Use your fist," Emma told her.

"What?" Julia wasn't sure what Emma said. Surely she couldn't have asked her to hit a fireball with her fist. Wouldn't she get burned? Wasn't that an extremely risky way of defeating this fiery mob? Julia looked over at Emma, who didn't have time to answer her question. Emma made a fist and struck the fireball, which flew back toward the blazes and destroyed one. You could use your fist to defeat the blaze, Julia thought, *and you don't get burned? That's awesome.*

A fireball flew toward her, and she put out her fist and cringed, worried the pain from the burn would overwhelm her and she'd pass out. She slammed her fist into the fireball, striking the ball that flew back toward the blaze, obliterating it.

They destroyed the two blazes, and continued their trip toward the Nether fortress, but were stopped by the entrance. Blazes guarded the fortress with great care, and aimed the fireballs at Emma and Julia with the intent of destroying them quickly.

"How did Hallie get past this on her own?" Julia gasped as she dodged one blast, and prepared to shield herself from the next.

The blazes lowered themselves and Emma slayed them with her sword. Emma was screaming at Julia, something about picking up what had been dropped.

"What?" Julia asked.

"The blaze rod," Emma said. "Pick it up. All of these drops are extremely valuable to Aaron and Mia. They help you brew very powerful and important potions." Emma added, "You have to help me, Julia. You can't be this passive. Just because you're a builder doesn't mean you don't have the capacity to learn other things."

Julia was offended. "You really hurt my feelings," she said as she took her first steps into the massive Nether fortress.

"I wasn't trying to hurt your feelings. I just want you to get accustomed to the Nether and to do it fast. This is a harsh biome and it takes a lot to survive here. I know you have what it takes, but you are just scared, that's all. Please don't be upset by it," Emma said.

"Okay," Julia replied. She didn't want to analyze the situation. She was too preoccupied with studying every inch of this Nether fortress. The Nether was the polar opposite of the snowy biome, where Julia was from. Where she lived, everything was icy and cold, but in the Nether, she feared she'd get burned if she touched anything. Julia paused by the stairs, pointing to a patch of deep red plant that sprouted next to the staircase, "What's this?"

"That's Nether wart. We should pick some. It's useful when feeding chickens and creating the awkward potion, but we have to do this fast. We don't have time to explore the Nether fortress and its many finds. We have to stop Hallie."

A voice boomed through the Fortress. "If you want to stop me, you came to the right place."

Julia stopped plucking the Nether wart and grabbed her bow and arrow, pointing it at Hallie who had appeared directly in front of them. "We are going to stop you, Hallie," Julia declared.

"How? With an arrow?" Hallie asked while pulling a potion from her inventory and taking a sip. "Now I'm very strong. Hit me, but you can't destroy me."

"Why are you doing this?" Julia asked as she flung an arrow at Hallie, but Hallie skillfully dodged the arrow and leaped toward Julia with a diamond sword she pulled from her inventory.

"It's a lot more fun to be evil." Hallie smiled as she plunged the sword deep into Julia's unprotected arm.

"Ouch!" Julia cried as the pain radiated down her left arm, and she dropped the arrow she was clutching with her right hand.

"Is it a lot more fun to be evil?" a voice called out.

Hallie was startled to see Lucy standing in front of her. Lucy pointed her diamond sword at Hallie. "So you weren't working alone, were you?"

"What?" Emma asked. "Who is she working with?"

Hallie struck Lucy with her sword. "I'm going to win," Hallie screamed as she pulled a potion out with the other hand and tossed the potent liquid on Emma and Julia, immobilizing them.

"Help—" Emma could barely get the words out as Hallie leaped toward her with a diamond sword.

Julia gathered enough strength to strike Hallie before she could destroy Emma. As Emma's energy returned, she grabbed a vial of potion and took a quick sip. Regaining her energy, she was able to strike Hallie with her sword.

Carla spawned in the center of the fortress, and Julia called out, "Carla! Help us battle Hallie."

"She won't help you," Lucy hollered as she struck Carla with her diamond sword. "She's working with Hallie."

"Why?" Julia asked again, but there was no reply. Carla was destroyed.

Emma and Julia slammed their swords into Hallie, destroying her with their powerful blows.

"We're safe." Julia sighed with relief.

"No, we're not," Emma grabbed her arm as an arrow pierced the exposed skin. "They're wither skeletons, Julia," she called out, identifying the hostile mob.

"What do we do?" Julia cried.

"I'll show you." Lucy lunged at the black block-headed skeleton with her diamond sword, knocking it back.

The second wither skeleton struck Julia with its sword before she had a moment to mobilize. Emma called out, "Drink milk!"

Julia weakly grabbed a bottle of milk from her inventory and took a sip. The milk helped her gather enough energy to strike the wither skeleton, which tumbled back against the wall of the Nether fortress. Emma raced over and struck the weakened wither skeleton with her diamond sword, destroying it. She picked up the piece of coal it dropped and handed it to Julia. "You deserve this."

An odd noise emanated from the hallway. Julia turned around and let out a terrified scream. It wasn't as loud as the scream in the Jungle prison, but it was still quite piercing and powerful. Emma said, "Please, Julia, stop."

"Magma cubes," Lucy gasped. "We don't have time to battle any more mobs, because we have to get back to campus. I'm afraid Hallie and Carla have taken over Minecrafters Academy by now."

Two voices called out in unison, "Don't worry! We can help!"

The trio looked over and saw Mia and Brad. They spawned in the center of the Nether fortress with full energy bars. Both energetically leapt at the magma cubes. Julia was hopeful they might get out of the Nether soon.

Chapter 16
SUNDOWN SURPRISES

Mia and Brad plunged their swords into the blocky cubes, as two blazes flew overhead.

"We have to get out of here," Lucy warned them. "Every minute we are away from the campus, we are putting the entire Academy in jeopardy. We must stop Hallie and Carla."

Julia closed her eyes as she plowed her sword into the wither skeleton. Even though fighting with your eyes closed was the worst fighting strategy, she couldn't bear to look at the menacing mob because they frightened her. The wither skeleton fell back as Emma raced to her side and destroyed it. "Open your eyes, Julia. It's over."

Julia opened her eyes as Lucy screamed, "Everyone outside! We must build a portal and get back to campus."

Brad and Mia were finishing up their two-person battle against the magma cubes, as Julia grabbed obsidian from her inventory and followed Lucy outside the Nether fortress.

"Is everyone here?" Lucy called out as she readied herself to ignite the portal.

"No," Julia replied. "Mia and Brad are still battling the magma cubes."

Brad hollered, "We're here. We defeated those pesky cubes."

Mia was out of breath. "That was intense."

"We have to get back to campus." Lucy made sure everyone was clustered together on the small portal before she ignited it.

Purple mist surrounded them. Julia grabbed a potion of strength as they traveled back to the campus. She knew she needed as much as energy as possible to defeat this evil duo that was overthrowing the campus.

The portal dropped them on the great lawn. Julia looked up at the sky and her heart beat fast as she saw night was approaching. It was already dark enough for hostile mobs to spawn. She knew they were in for a rough night as three zombies lumbered toward them.

Emma was the first to strike the vacant-eyed mobs, annihilating one of the mobs with her diamond sword. Brad rushed to her side to battle the remaining zombies. Julia was going to join them when she spotted Hallie sprinting past her. Julia raced toward Hallie.

"Stop!" Julia called out as an arrow struck her leg. She turned around and saw Carla standing in front of her with a bow and arrow.

"You're not going anywhere," Carla threatened.

Four skeletons spawned behind Carla. Julia didn't warn her. She just stood in silence as the bony beasts aimed their arrows at Carla and flooded her with a barrage of arrows. Carla was gone, but Hallie was still terrorizing the campus. She was striking Mia with her diamond sword when Hallie sprinted over and leaped at Julia.

"Stop destroying our school!" Julia screamed as she plunged her sword deep into every limb that wasn't covered by Hallie's diamond armor. Hallie's knee-high socks dropped to her ankles as Julia struck her roommate. "This has to stop!"

Lucy rushed over, delivering the final blow, destroying Hallie. "She must have respawned in your room. We have to trap her. The only way this battle will be over is if we place both Hallie and Carla in a bedrock prison. Julia, you must start constructing the prison. It's our only hope."

Julia didn't have enough bedrock in her inventory to build a prison, but she knew someone who had a large supply. She sprinted toward Brad as the sun came up.

"Brad," Julia said breathlessly. "I need your help." She told Brad Lucy's plan, and he gathered bedrock from his inventory.

"I have a great idea for the design," Brad said.

Julia didn't want to admit that she enjoyed this project, and she really liked working with Brad to construct the prison. They created the foundation and worked tirelessly to finish the prison while they waited for Lucy to deliver the first criminals.

"I heard there used to be a bedrock prison on this campus before," Brad said.

"Really?"

"Aaron told me about a corrupt headmaster who was once housed on the campus, along with various griefers."

"That's awful. I wonder what happened to them," Julia said as they placed a door on the prison.

"I think that was ages ago and they were released," Brad said. "I don't know what happened to the original prison, though."

Julia wanted Aaron to tell her tales of Minecrafters Academy and its history, but she also knew that she was in the middle of creating history at Minecrafters Academy as they placed the door and finished the bedrock jail.

Julia heard someone call for help. With a concerned expression, she looked over at Brad. "It sounds like Lucy!"

Chapter 17
BACK TO CLASS

"Help!" Lucy cried out again.

Julia and Brad sprinted toward the sounds of Lucy's cries as they pulled their swords from their inventory, ready to attack Carla and Hallie.

"I think the cries are coming from in here." Julia led Brad into the dorms, and they raced into Julia's room.

Brad opened the door to find Lucy surrounded by Carla and Hallie. Brad pounced on Hallie as she dropped her sword.

Julia knew that destroying Hallie was useless. She just had to weaken her enough to get her into the prison.

Aaron, Emma, Henry, and Mia sprinted into the room. Aaron declared with excitement, "We have removed every brick of TNT from the campus."

"What?" Carla was infuriated and struck Lucy with her diamond sword in anger.

"It's over," Aaron said. "You're outnumbered."

"Did you complete the prison?" Lucy asked. Her voice was weak and after the last blow from Carla, she barely had enough energy to stand.

"Yes," Brad replied. "Julia and I finished it."

"Do you seriously think you're going to keep me behind bars?" Hallie laughed as she struck Lucy with her sword. Lucy cried in pain.

"Yes." Aaron walked up to Hallie and splashed a potion of weakness on her as Mia doused Carla with a potion.

Julia pointed her sword at Hallie. "Follow me. You have a new home now."

Hallie and Carla knew the battle was over, and reluctantly followed Julia out of the dorms and toward the bedrock building.

Everyone stood on the great lawn and watched as Hallie and Carla marched across the grass and into the bedrock prison. As Hallie and Carla took their final steps of freedom, Hallie called out to the crowd of students and faculty, "This isn't over. I promise you it's far from over."

"I'm sorry, but it is over," Lucy said as she closed the door of the bedrock prison and announced to the students and faculty, "Thank you all for helping us defeat these criminals. They intended to turn this prestigious academy into a place where people would be taught to be evil. I'm glad that we were able to save Minecrafters Academy. This is a great day in our school's history."

The crowd cheered as Lucy continued. "We must spend the next few days rebuilding, but then we will be back to class."

Julia worked on constructed the dining hall, alongside Brad. As they finished the construction of the dining hall, she began to focus on the Academic Olympics. She wondered if the school was still going to participate after the antics that had taken place on campus. She also wondered if she would be chosen. After working with Brad, she knew they were equally skilled, and it would be a tough decision for the faculty to choose between them. She wished they could both go, but she knew that wasn't going to happen. Only one person could represent the Academy in each subject.

When all of the buildings were completed, Lucy held an assembly in the new auditorium. Everyone on campus gathered in the assembly as Lucy stepped behind a shiny new wooden podium. "Classes will resume tomorrow."

The crowd cheered again.

"I have a special announcement. We have chosen the students for the Minecraft Academic Olympics."

The auditorium was silent.

"It was a tough decision. As you know, I feel everyone at the school is incredibly skilled, but these are the students the faculty has chosen to represent the school."

There was not a sound in the room. Julia held her breath. This was the minute she was both excited for and equally dreading.

"Mia," Julia called out. "Please come up to the podium."

Mia walked up to the podium, and Lucy said, "You are chosen to represent Minecrafters Academy as an alchemist."

"Thank you." Mia's eyes filled with tears. "I'm so honored to be chosen. I will try my hardest to represent the school."

Mia stood next to Lucy as she called out the second name. "Emma."

Julia was thrilled both of her friends were chosen. She hoped she'd be next, but she looked over at Brad and also wished he might be the one asked to participate in the competition.

Lucy announced, "Emma will represent the school as a warrior. She will prove that she's a skilled fighter in the Academic Olympics." Emma thanked Lucy, and everyone collectively held their breath as they waited for Lucy to announce the final name.

Chapter 18
ACADEMIC OLYMPICS

Julia didn't walk up to the podium when Lucy called her name. She didn't believe her name was called, and she stood in the crowd.

"Julia," Lucy repeated.

It was then Julia finally realized her name was really called. She hated standing in front of a crowd, and shook as she approached the podium. This should have been her moment of glory, but she wasn't a fan of attention. She preferred to be behind the scenes. Standing next to Lucy in front of the assembly, she thanked everyone on the faculty. Julia took a deep breath and smiled. She looked over at her two friends. Their dream had come true; they were going to represent the school in the Minecraft Academic Olympics.

The assembly was over and Brad made his way over to Julia, "Congratulations," he said.

"Thanks." Julia smiled.

"You're going to blow away all the other builders in the Overworld," Brad told her.

Emma sprinted over to Julia. "I can't believe we're going together."

Mia exclaimed, "How awesome!"

Julia felt bad for Brad as he stood next to them and overheard the trio discussing their excitement for being chosen to represent the school. Students and faculty approached them and wished them luck and congratulations.

Mia and Julia noticed Aaron standing at the back of the auditorium, talking to Lucy. They walked toward him. "I'm sorry to interrupt," Mia said, "but I was wondering if Aaron could help me practice for the competition."

"Funny you should ask that," Lucy said as she smiled, "Aaron, can you tell them what we were discussing?"

"I accepted a position at the Academy. I'm going to teach alchemy," he said.

"Wow, that's amazing." Mia sounded excited to study with Aaron.

Emma ran over to the group as Aaron told them about his new job. "I can't wait to teach you how to brew various potions."

Henry walked over. "I will teach you how to survive when you're on the hunt for the ingredients."

Max overheard their discussion. "And I'm still going to get you to make the best mods ever."

Julia looked at her teachers and friends. She knew she'd try her best when they were at the competition, but she also knew that once she returned, she'd be able to learn from both the faculty and students at Minecrafters Academy. It was a long journey from her solitary life in the snowy biome, and she was certainly glad she made it. No matter what the outcome of the competition was, she had already learned so much in her new life.

READ ON FOR AN EXCITING SNEAK PEEK AT THE NEXT BOOK IN

Winter Morgan's Unofficial Minecrafters Academy series

Available wherever books are sold in June 2017
From Sky Pony Press

Chapter 1
SPECIAL GUESTS

J ulia's heart skipped a beat when she walked underneath the gate that stood at the entrance to Minecrafters Academy. This was her second year at the school, but she still had a tinge of excitement as she entered the campus. Julia was particularly happy because this year, students were allowed to choose their roommates. After sharing a dorm room with Hallie, Julia was thrilled at the opportunity to pick her bunkmate, but there was one problem: she wanted to choose both Emma and Mia, but she could only pick one roommate.

"What are we going to do?" Julia asked her friends as they stood outside the dorm.

Lucy stood in the middle of a group of students and called out, "Everyone stand next to the person you'd like to be your roommate."

Julia looked over at Emma and Mia, who stood next to each other. She felt left out, and scanned the area for another friend who might want to room with her. Julia searched through the crowd, but there was nobody. Emma moved closer to Julia and whispered, "We want to be with you. Let's just stick together and see if we can all share a room."

Julia smiled. She knew her friends cared about her, but it was always tricky when three people were involved.

Lucy walked over to Julia, Mia, and Emma. "Would all three of you like to share a room? There's an oversized room that has three beds. I can offer that to you."

Julia unleashed the loudest sigh of relief and looked over at her two friends. Emma had already answered yes.

"Great." Lucy led them to the corner room with four windows.

Mia rushed to the windows, gazing at the panoramic view of the great lawn, dining hall, and other campus buildings. "We have the best views of Minecrafters Academy. Thanks, Lucy."

"All three of you were so helpful to the school last year and I wanted to make sure you were rewarded."

Emma hesitated. "But we didn't win the Minecraft Academic Olympics." Tears filled Emma's eyes. "We are a disappointment to the school, and it's all my fault."

"It's not your fault," Lucy comforted Emma. "You were skilled enough to be chosen. The Minecraft Academic Olympics is a tough competition. We should be proud that our school was even chosen to participate in it."

Emma said, "But I lost the battle. I came in last."

Julia walked over to Emma. "You are a skilled fighter and a teacher."

"A teacher?" Emma asked.

"When I came to Minecrafters Academy, I didn't even know how to use my sword. I'd freeze every time I'd encounter a zombie or a skeleton, but you taught how to fight and to be brave."

"Really?" Emma dried her eyes.

Lucy said, "I must excuse myself. I have to meet my friend Steve. He's going to be a guest teacher here this year."

Mia's eyes lit up. "What will he teach? I want to move past alchemy and try something else."

"Farming. Steve is one of the best farmers in the Overworld," Lucy explained and then exited the room.

Mia spoke as she decorated her wall with emeralds. "I'm glad there will be a good farming class. I might consider becoming a farmer. Once school is over, I can live on a small farm and sell potions."

A sweat grew on Julia's brow. She hadn't thought about what she'd do after graduation. They had another year left of school, and she was just enjoying being back on campus. She assumed she'd just go back to the cold biome. However, when she came in first place at the Minecraft Academic Olympics, people from the Olympic Committee asked Julia if she'd build various structures in the Overworld. During the summer break, Julia didn't return to the cold biome, and instead spent the school break constructing a tree house that someone had commissioned her to build. Julia knew she could be a builder when she graduated, and this thought comforted her as she organized her section of the room.

Emma spent a long time in the closet, and Julia called out, "Emma, are you okay?"

Emma chuckled. "Yes, I was just inspecting every inch of that closet. After finding Hallie's closet filled with TNT, I was worried there would be something sinister in this one."

"Well," Mia asked, "is there?"

"No." Emma smiled. "It's just a plain old closet and we should fill it with our chests."

The group carefully placed their chests on the closet floor as they heard footsteps approaching their room.

"Who's there?" Julia's heart raced. Even though all of the excitement from last year was over and the school was rebuilt, Julia was still on edge.

"It's Brad," he answered and stepped inside. "Are you guys here?"

"Yes." Julia was excited to see her old friend. "How are you, Brad?"

"Hungry. It's the First Night Back Dinner. Do you guys want to go?"

Emma rushed to the window. "Wow, I didn't realize how late it was. It looks as if the dinner has already begun."

They walked toward the dinner as Julia told Brad about her summer and the tree house.

"You know what I had to build this summer?" Brad asked.

"No, what?" Julia replied.

"An igloo. I wanted to contact you for help, but I knew you were working on the tree house."

"You should have asked me to help you. I love building igloos," Julia said.

Emma interrupted. "This is the most lavish dinner I've ever attended," she said as she pointed at the tables of pork chops, beef, chicken, carrots, potatoes, watermelon, apples, cakes, and cookies. "This is nicer than a holiday meal."

Mia wasn't concerned with the food. She wanted to find Steve to ask him if she could volunteer to work on the school farm. She noticed someone she didn't recognize talking to Lucy, Henry, Max, and Aaron. Mia walked over to them, assuming it must be Steve.

Lucy said, "Mia, this is our new visiting teacher, Steve.'"

Mia introduced herself, explaining that she would love to be considered to volunteer for the farm.

"I thought you were an alchemist," Aaron said.

"I am," Mia replied. "But I'd like to increase my skill set, and farming really interests me."

"I'd love to teach you," Steve said. "It's so nice to see someone who cares about farming. Tomorrow I'm teaching a class on farming."

"That's on my schedule," Mia said.

"After the class, you can join me on the school farm. I'm looking for other volunteers, too, if you know of any students who might be interested."

Mia didn't have a chance to reply. Two block-carrying lanky Endermen made their way toward her. One looked at Mia and let out a high-pitched shriek. Mia cried out for help as the Enderman teleported toward her. Her heart was racing. She was trapped.

Chapter 2
DOWN THE HOLE

"Run toward the pond!" Lucy called out to a scared and frozen Mia.

Mia stared at the pond as the Enderman struck her. She was shaking and wasn't sure she could make it.

"You can do it!" Emma shook as she lunged toward the Enderman with her diamond sword.

Mia was in utter shock. She looked down at her feet, which seemed to have a life of their own as they sprinted toward the small pond. The Enderman was on her trail, and she could feel the purple-eyed creature reach for her and she knew her only chance of survival was jumping into the water. The water splashed her face as the lanky Enderman fell into the water. The water instantly destroyed the block-carrying mob, and Mia was safe. As she stepped out of the pond, Emma and Julia stood on the grass.

"It's getting dark." Emma looked up at the sky. "Let's head back before more hostile mobs appear."

"Really? You never want to head home at dusk. Last year you used to stay up all night to see what mobs you'd encounter. You usually love battling hostile mobs," Mia reminded her.

"Yeah," Julia said. "Didn't you destroy a chicken jockey on your own?'

"That was last year," Emma replied as they walked back to the dorm.

"Is this because of the Olympics? I feel like ever since that competition you haven't been yourself," Mia said.

"I just helped you battle an Enderman, didn't I?" Emma was annoyed. She didn't want her friends analyzing why she wasn't fighting.

Mia said, "Yes, but I just sense that you don't enjoy fighting anymore."

"Maybe I'll become a farmer with you," Emma said.

Students were leaving the First Night Back Dinner as the trio weaved their way through the crowd and walked across the great lawn in the direction of their room.

Mia said, "Emma, I'd love for you to farm with me. In fact, Steve told me he needs volunteers for his farm."

"I'll do it," Emma replied.

"Me too. I'd be up for learning how to farm," Julia said.

"Great. Tomorrow, we will meet Steve after class to work on the farm," Mia said.

The girls crawled into their beds and said goodnight. In the dark room, Julia covered herself in a blue wool blanket and said, "I'm really happy we were able to get a room together."

"Me too," Emma said with a yawn.

* * * *

The next morning, Mia called out to them. "Wake up. We don't want to be late for Steve's Farming class."

"Five more minutes," begged a sleepy Emma.

"What about breakfast?" Julia asked. "Do we have time to eat? I'm starving."

"No, we overslept." Mia handed Julia and apple. "Eat this."

"What about me?" Emma asked as she slowly sat up in the bed.

"This is my last apple." Mia handed it to Emma. "We should pick some at the school farm. Are you guys ready?"

Julia and Emma walked alongside Mia to Steve's class. Emma took a bite out of her apple.

"You have to finish that apple before class," Mia said. "I want us to make a good impression."

"Don't worry," Emma said. "We will."

The trio entered the class. Julia knew Hallie was in the bedrock prison on campus, yet she still searched for her face in the classroom.

Steve entered the class and asked, "Has anyone ever built a farm?"

Shockingly only a few people raised their hands. A boy with orange hair said, "I've spent my entire life on a farm."

"Great." Steve smiled. "You will be very helpful to the class. What's your name?"

"Nick."

Another student with rusty brown hair raised his hand. "Do I really have to be here? Farming is so lame."

"Lame? Do you like eating potatoes and having wheat?" Steve asked the student.

"Yes," he replied.

"You can't have any of those things without a farm." Steve lectured the class on how farms are vital to everyone's survival in the Overworld. He taught them the basics of farming. "Before anything you must have a seed stock."

As Steve spoke, Mia took meticulous notes. She wanted to learn every aspect of farming. As the class came to a close, Steve announced, "I'm looking for a few volunteers to help on the school farm. If you're interested, please meet me by the school farm following the class."

Mia looked over at her friends and smiled. She enjoyed being in the class, but she was eager to get into the dirt and start planting. She also wanted to replenish her supply of apples.

Class was over, and Julia walked over to her friends. "What's up with the guy who told Steve farming was lame? That was incredibly rude."

"Yes," Mia agreed.

The trio entered the school farm, and Julia was shocked to see the boy from class who dismissed farming, standing next to Steve.

Steve looked at the group of volunteers, which included Mia, Emma, Julia, Nick and the boy with rusty brown hair. Steve asked the boy to introduce himself.

"I'm Jamie."

Steve held a pickaxe and dug in into a patch of dirt. "We have to start building an irrigation system."

"Yes, crops can't grow without water," Nick said.

"Very good, Nick," Steve remarked as he dug deeper, but paused.

"What is it? Can we not dig here?" Nick asked.

"No." Steve stared inside the hole he had dug. "We can, but—"

"Then what is it?" Nick questioned. "Why did you stop?"

Steve leaned over the hole and pulled out a large treasure chest.

"Cool," Jamie exclaimed.

Steve cleaned the dirt off the top of the chest and opened it. "Diamonds."

Julia looked inside. "And enchanted books."

"I wonder who this belongs to," Mia said.

Julia assumed it belonged to Hallie or some other criminal that was hiding their treasures, but also wondered, "Do you think this could have spawned naturally?"

"Possibly," Steve replied. "Since you were all here when we found it, I think everyone in the group should share the loot from the treasure."

"Wow!" Julia exclaimed. "That's awesome."

As Steve picked up the first diamond from the chest, a powerful thunderous boom shook the campus.